A WALK PAST ELLEN'S HOUSE

A WALK PAST ELLEN'S HOUSE

by Syd Hoff

McGraw-Hill Book Company

New York • St. Louis • San Francisco • Montreal • Panama • Toronto

Other books by Syd Hoff:
ROBERTO AND THE BULL
THE LITTER KNIGHT

Library of Congress Cataloging in Publication Data

Hoff, Sydney,
   A walk past Ellen's house.

   SUMMARY: Harvey wants to walk past a special girl's
house but he's afraid the other boys will laugh.
   I.   Title.
PZ7.H672Wal   [E]   72-11751
ISBN 0-07-029175-6
ISBN 0-07-029176-4 (lib. bdg.)

1234567890 HDBP 79876543

Harvey wanted to take a walk past Ellen's
house. He wanted to see Ellen. He wanted
Ellen to see him.

But Harvey was afraid the other boys on the street would know why he went there. He was afraid they would laugh at him and let her know.

So Harvey stayed where he was, down at
the other end of the street. He never took a
walk past Ellen's house.

"Here's money. Get me a loaf of bread at
the bake shop," said Harvey's mother.

Harvey went to the bake shop, but he went
four blocks out of the way.

Even coming back with the bread, as tired
as Harvey was, he didn't dare take a walk past
Ellen's house.

"Let's play follow the leader," said the other boys on the street.

Harvey followed them past the Kelly house,
the Goldberg house, the Cavello house—

—but he always turned around and started back before he'd have to take a walk past Ellen's house.

"Hey, Harvey, come on and follow us!
What's the idea turning around and starting
back?" asked the other boys.

"Aw, who wants to play," Harvey would
say. Or, "I just remembered I have to do
something."

Then he'd stay in front of his own house
with nothing to do.

"Daddy's coming home, way up the street,"
his mother would say. "Run and meet him."

Harvey would wait just where he was to
meet his father.

Then he'd stay in his room until it got late
and kept telling himself that tomorrow he
would *really* take a walk past Ellen's house.

But the next day and the next, Harvey just
stayed in front of his own house, and kept
saying the same thing.

One day the boys on Harvey's street started
playing a game of ball.

"Catch the ball, Harvey!" they shouted.

Harvey ran after the ball, all the way up the street toward Ellen's house.

"I'll show Ellen what a good catcher I am," he thought.

Then Harvey thought, "Suppose I don't catch the ball. Suppose Ellen sees me miss it."

He stopped chasing the ball!

"Why didn't you keep chasing it?" the boys asked.

"Aw, he's afraid to let Ellen see him," one of them said.

All the boys laughed. Harvey went back to
his own house. He knew he'd never have the
nerve to do it. He'd never have the nerve to
do anything.

Just then he saw a lady all the way up the street. She was coming home from the market, loaded with heavy shopping bags.

"Wait for me!" Harvey shouted.

He ran up the street, past Ellen's house,
to help the lady home with her shopping bags.

After that, Harvey sat down and thought, "Gee, I took a walk past Ellen's house just now because somebody needed me. Well, maybe Ellen needs me too. Maybe she needs me to be her friend, just like I need her to be mine."

He was never afraid to take a walk past
Ellen's house again.